The Snow

Dragon

Leyla Howard

Limited Special Edition. No. 18 of 20 Paperbacks

Leyla Howard is a qualified primary school teacher. She lives in Cumbria with her partner and sons. She has worked in schools in London where she realised how important stories are in helping children develop and play. Her inspiration for writing is her sons, her family and all of the children she has taught over the years who have made story time special.

lots of love from
Leyla Howard -
x

The Snow

Dragon

Leyla Howard

AUSTIN MACAULEY PUBLISHERS™

LONDON ★ CAMBRIDGE ★ NEW YORK ★ SHARJAH

A CIP catalogue record for this title is available from the British Library.

ISBN 9781786932518 (Paperback)
ISBN 9781528952903 (ePub e-book)
www.austinmacauley.com

First Published (2019)
Austin Macauley Publishers Ltd
25 Canada Square
Canary Wharf
London
E14 5LQ

To Caius and Callan, for teaching me there is joy and magic in every day.

To Liam, for encouraging me to follow my dreams.

To Mum, Dad, Nadia and Kam, for your unconditional love and support.

With thanks to Liam and Mum for their input and ideas.

"Uniqueness"

ju:ˈniːknəs/

*the quality of being the only one of its kind.

*the quality of being particularly remarkable, special, or unusual

(Source: Google Dictionary, 2017)

Up in the mountains where the trees touch the sky, lived a family of dragons who soared ever so high.

They would race to the stars; in the clouds they would swim.

With the whip of a tail and the flap of a wing.

As the dragons practiced their roar, the forest echoed and swayed. But for one little dragon, things weren't going his way.

This sweet little dragon, unlike the others, was not like his parents, his sisters or brothers.

He arched his back, dug his claws in the ground. But instead of a roar came a trumpety sound.

The dragons collapsed with laughter, then roared fiercely, calling him names. "You are different!" they exclaimed, the little dragon was ashamed.

Now as everyone knows, all dragons breathe fire. It is something that comes natural and is much so required.

But our little dragon, with every blow, could not breathe fire...and instead breathed SNOW!

"We will call you snow dragon!" cried his siblings as they mocked. They stretched their wings and took flight as the little dragon flopped.

The snow dragon felt sad, "I don't fit in here, all of the other dragons breathe fire and fear."

Under the light of the moon, shadowed by the trees, he set off for a place he would feel more at ease.

Wandering, he practiced his fire-breathing blow. But oh no, oh no, all that followed was snow.

Living snug in the forest, there is a village so serene. If you ever were to visit, it may feel like a dream.

With perfect thatched roofs and picket fences to surround, even the butterflies dance as they kiss flowers in the ground.

Now the villagers kept their distance as the old stories would tell, that dragons and villagers don't mix very well. Naughty Noostiba, the nuisance baker (most people knew him as a troublemaker), had left on his oven whilst having a nap, and oh my goodness when he came back; a commotion had started as flames scorched and leapt. The street had caught fire whilst he had slept.

The villagers cried for help as the flames spread, they grabbed their children from their homes and fled. The mayor called for water, but the rivers and lakes had gone. The birds in the trees flocked, there was no merry song. Meanwhile in the distance the snow dragon walked on. "I am no good to anyone."

Sitting down by a log a tear fell from his eye, "Why can't I roar, breathe fire or fly high?"

A squirrel scurried past, followed by a family of mice. "Why dragon don't just sit there, take my advice. The forest is burning, make a start and run, head down the mountain with everyone."

All of a sudden, there were badgers and bears, cubs being carried, the animals looked scared.

Snow dragon looked back. "The forest IS burning!" The flames leapt higher, jumping and turning.

His heart raced fast, pounding like a drum. "My forest, my family, my dad and my mum!" And just like that, his feet pushed off the ground. The trees shook, the animals heard a new roaring sound. Before he could think, the little dragon was in flight. He flapped his wings and roared with might.

From his strong wide jaws came not only a roar, but a blanket of snow crystals began to pour.

The burning forest withered under the icy flakes. The dragons and villagers cried, "This must be a mistake!?"

Together they blinked and gazed through the billowing smoke. The dragons, forest animals and village folk. Floating high above them was a magnificent sight. Wings as wide as a plane in flight.

A puffed out chest followed by a deafening roar, the snow dragon smiled as he effortlessly soared.

The village mayor clapped his hands with relief and cheers echoed from the forest to the streets. "You saved us brave dragon!" The villagers exclaimed. "Tell us oh tell us, what is your name?"

The snow dragon's family looked rather ashamed but the dragon just grinned and said, "Snow dragon IS my name."

Since that day, villagers and dragons live in harmony, because the truly best parts of us are the ones we can't see. There is always a way you can help, always something you can do. There is a hero in all of us. There is a hero in you!